You Are Enough

Cassandra,

Thank you for sharing your gifts + talents with the world!

Continued Blessings!

You Are Enough

A Guide to Love, Joy, Peace, Freedom and Acceptance

Jacqueline Hayes

Copyright © 2013 by Jacqueline Hayes.

Library of Congress Control Number:		2013913419
ISBN:	Hardcover	978-1-4836-8129-0
	Softcover	978-1-4836-8128-3
	Ebook	978-1-4836-8130-6

All rights reserved. No part of this book may be reproduced or transmitted in any form or by any means, electronic or mechanical, including photocopying, recording, or by any information storage and retrieval system, without permission in writing from the copyright owner.

This book was printed in the United States of America.

Rev. date: 09/13/2013

To order additional copies of this book, contact:
Xlibris LLC
1-888-795-4274
www.Xlibris.com
Orders@Xlibris.com

Contents

Preface ix
Acknowledgments xiii
Introduction xv

Chapter 1: You Are Special 1
Chapter 2: Wake Up, Pay Attention, Ask the Hard Questions 17
Chapter 3: I Am Not Your Opinion of Me 31
Chapter 4: Dream Big / Burn the Boat / Have Faith 43
Chapter 5: Value / Guard Your Time 63
Conclusion 75
About the Author 77
Index 79

This book is dedicated to every woman. May you discover the precious gem within.

> You are beautiful.
>
> You are special.
>
> You are brilliant.
>
> You are unique.
>
> You are love.
>
> You are loved.

that you are divine, you are unique, you are special, you are brilliant, you are love, and you are loved. My hope is that this book will provide hope, inspiration, courage, and insight on how to live the best life you desire to live starting today—starting right now. My deepest desire is that this book will serve as an awakening, serve as an invitation to embark upon your personal journey of self-discovery.

My beloved sister, my friend, may you discover who you are, why you are here, and what you should be doing with your life. I wrote this book for you. I wrote this book for every woman who finds herself in a place in her life where she is searching for more—more meaning, more joy, more substance, more love, more freedom, and more vitality in life. I wrote this book with you in mind. May the words of this book ignite a flame in your spirit, a fire in your soul, and a yearning in your heart that will impel you to take a leap of faith into the unknown, a walk down the road less traveled, a dance with the devil in the darkness to reclaim your soul, and a crossing over from the wilderness into your promised land—a land filled with beauty, love, wonder, joy, abundance, and excitement.

My beloved sister, please know you were born for a specific purpose, your life matters. Your thoughts and ideas are important, valued, and needed to make this world a better, more peaceful, and more loving place. No matter where you are in your life right now, no matter what is going on at this present moment, know that all things are working together for your good if you will allow them to.

As you are reading this book, my hope is that you will discover that you are your biggest obstacle to overcome. You are the only person standing in the way of you experiencing the life you desire. You must find the courage to let love in and let go of the negative thoughts of your past. You must figure out how to get out of your own way. You have the power to change your life.

Preface

To get the most out of this book, my request is that you read this book with an open mind and a strong personal desire to take responsibility for your life. Consider this book as an offering, an invitation, an opportunity. Consider this book as a gift that gives you permission to fully embrace and accept the person, the woman you are. During or after reading this book, my hope is that you will come to understand that the woman you are is the woman you were created to be. My hope is that you will learn to recognize your uniqueness and appreciate your beauty. I also hope you will come to understand that there are no misplaced parts, no ill-fitted features or improperly placed qualities about you. You were uniquely and wonderfully made. You are a masterpiece. Everything about you is as it should be—every freckle, every mole, every curve, and every hair. May you allow yourself to open up and experience freedom in your mind and spirit. May the shackles of guilt, shame, and regret be destroyed and broken off your life. May you come to fully understand that you are not your past. May the words in this book inspire you, encourage you, challenge you, heal you, and more importantly, motivate you to seek the truth—the truth

You Are Enough

Everything you need to change your life is already in your possession. It begins with renewing your mind. Wake up and pay attention to the thoughts you are allowing to occupy your mental space. Everything that has happened and is happening in your life has led you to this point, to this crossroads. This is a beautiful and magnificent moment in your life. The direction you take from this day will determine the next course of your life. If you choose to remain where you are and do nothing, many people will miss being healed and restored because you are too afraid to choose, too afraid to let go of what is not working for you, and too afraid to trust your spirit, to trust your inner guide.

You were led to this book because deep inside, you are secretly crying for change, healing, and release. You are acutely aware that you are miserable in your life. You are very clear that you are unhappy and unfulfilled in your life and in your relationships. Yet you continue to wear the mask and travel down the same path of suffering, neglect, deprivation, and abuse. Deep inside, you feel the urge, the tug, and the quiet whisper that is inviting you to take the journey within. You continue to ignore the call and avoid the whisper that is inviting you to let go of the pain, let go of your past, and walk into your destiny.

Today is your day. Your life has shifted, and events have ordered your steps to this moment in your life. The invitation has been extended. It is awaiting your acceptance. It will not force you to take it or demand that you give it a try; however, the invitation is always there for you, gently knocking at your heart.

My hope is that at some point during your reading of this book, you will answer the call, accept the invitation, release the fear, let go and surrender in faith, and surrender to love. My sincerest desire is that you will discover that you are everything you were created to be. Nothing is wrong with you. Your Creator did not make a mistake with you. You are special. You are unique. You are love. You are loved. You are enough.

Before diving in and embarking upon this journey, I would like to offer this healing-soup recipe as a way of softening your spirit and soothing your soul to accept whatever is necessary for you to make the shift, face your fears, ask the hard questions, forgive those who have violated or hurt you, embrace change, experience healing, and walk in love and wholeness. The ingredients of the healing soup work together in harmony to heal all areas within. Bon appétit!

Healing Soup Recipe

1 cup of acceptance
2 tablespoons of release
2 cups of forgiveness
1 ounce of hope
1 tablespoon of time
a pinch of faith
lots of love

Mix all ingredients together in your spirit; let simmer as long as necessary. When ready, serve and enjoy a new quality of life.

Acknowledgments

To every person who has crossed my path and led me to this place in my life, thank you. For the challenging, difficult, uncomfortable, and heart-wrenching situations that have allowed the beautiful goddess within to emerge, thank you. For the way I have been cracked open and set free from the burden of guilt, shame, and regret, thank you. For the gift of this bright, illuminating light that shines from within, thank you. For this vast open space inside me with infinite power, wisdom, and love, thank you.

To my best girls Kellie, Sharmon, and Shawna, thank you for your friendship.

To my amazing friend Carlos, thank you for your friendship.

To my cool friend Louis, thank you for being a great listener and a good friend.

To my cousin Robin, the Thelma to my Louise, the best cousin a person could ask for, thank you for always being so real and so cool.

To the three people who have always believed in me, supported me, and given me the confidence, freedom, and courage to live, discover my wings, and fly—thank you to my mother, Laura Hayes, and my two brothers, Willie and Dedric Hayes. I am who I am because of you and your love for me. Your love has been and continues to be the wind beneath my wings.

To my Creator, for this beautiful and amazing gift called life and for the wonderful discoveries I have experienced in my life thus far, thank you. For this person—this woman—I have discovered within, thank you.

Introduction

In this book, I will discuss a few principles and concepts that will, hopefully, help women make the shift from outward roaming to inward living. My hope is that this book will inspire women to discover who they are—their beauty, their charm, their amazing abilities, and their uniqueness. I hope the concepts shared in this book will offer women the opportunity to take a look at themselves from the inside out and discover that who they are is who they're meant to be and to know that their Creator made them perfect just as they are.

I believe once this shift has occurred, it will open the door for so many new things to be discovered, such as love, strength, wisdom, compassion, and sexiness. May you give yourself permission to accept and to surrender to this moment. Your life is about to change.

At the end of each chapter, you will find a personal declaration—a commitment you can make to yourself to support you on your journey of healing, growth, and change. Enjoy the journey!

CHAPTER 1

You Are Special

The day you were born, your Creator smiled with joy and love and said to the world, "Today is a great day. Look at my precious, beautiful child. She is going to do great things in the world. I have buried magnificent treasures inside her. There are diamonds buried in her innermost secret parts. She is my precious pearl, my beautiful, rare jewel. She is royalty. She belongs to a legacy of greatness. The world will be a better place because of her.

"She is my beloved, my special gift to the world. She is my divine masterpiece. When I look at her, I weep with joy and gladness. I say to myself, 'What a beautiful girl.' She is wrapped and clothed in love. She wears the garments of grace, pride, joy, peace, confidence, compassion, patience, and power.

"Whatever she needs, I am here for her. I will be right by her side every step of the way. When she calls, I will answer. When she asks, she will receive. When she knocks, I will open the door for her. I love her. She is special to me.

"My grace and love will cover her. My compassion and wisdom will order her steps. Wherever she goes, there will I be also. I will protect her, guard her, bless her, love her, and endow her with power, creativity, and passion. She will never be alone. I will always be right by her side to provide her every need."

What if every little girl were whispered these words every night before she went to bed? Just imagine how many amazing women there would be in the world today.

I believe life is a gift that has been given to us to discover, unfold, and enjoy. With the gift of life is the wisdom necessary to get us through the journey. The reason that I know life is a gift is that I did not ask to come here. I did not put in a special request to God/Spirit to come here. Many moons ago, a power that is so great and so awesome saw fit for my parents to have a heavenly exchange as husband and wife (Mommy/Daddy time, wink, wink), and as a result, I was conceived. To me, that is magical and so amazing. My physical form is a coalescence of my mother and my father; however, I am my own person. No one owns me but the Source that created me. The ground that I walk on is sacred because of the people who have sacrificed in many different ways so that I may experience the plethora of freedoms I enjoy in my life.

This life I have been given is a special and sacred gift. All the gifts and treasures that are wrapped up inside me were meant to be discovered and intended to bless the world. I was created to serve and to be of service. The gifts that have been planted inside me are intended to be given out and shared with the world. I have a duty and a responsibility to do my part in making the world a better place than I found it. I have an assignment to fulfill.

I believe it is our birthright to enjoy this gift called life—to live, learn, laugh, grow, and love. Love ourselves and love one another. I believe we are all the same. I believe we are created from the same Source. Each person is special and unique. I believe we were created for a purpose that is connected to the Source that gave us life. I cannot explain everything, nor do I try to figure everything out. I believe the figuring-out part is God's job, and since He knows everything, nothing is unfamiliar or out of order to Him. I believe my assignment is to live, be alive (present and aware), love, and love some more until my cycle of life evolves into its next phase.

There is something very sexy about a woman who knows who she is. Regardless of the situation or circumstances she finds herself in, she remains strong and resilient. This intangible quality is very palpable when she is in your presence. Her presence commands respect because she respects herself. This type of woman does not seek validation or security from others. She knows who she is. She knows that the One who created her created her exactly as she should be. She does not brag or boast. She simply walks in the essence of who she is. She walks with the understanding that she is a divine masterpiece, perfectly sculpted and designed by her Creator. Every angle, every curve is exactly as it should be.

Sadly, today, many women are walking around totally unaware of their beauty and awesomeness. Many women are thinking and believing thoughts about themselves that are completely opposite of who they truly are. This is unfortunate! Here is a footnote to remember: what you think about yourself is the only belief that is true for you, not necessarily the truth. The beliefs you have formed in your mind have been coded as truths. These false truths influence what you believe about yourself and your reality. Many of our beliefs are shaped by the experiences and situations we have witnessed or experienced when we were little girls. Whether the experiences were positive, healthy, pleasant, or otherwise, those experiences created imprints in our spirit and left remnants in our thoughts about who we believe we are and what we think we can do and the lens through which we view the world and our relationships.

When I was a little girl, my father called me his special flower, his petunia. He was the center of my universe. My father always made me feel special and loved. He always made me feel like I was the most important person in the world. My dad was tall, quiet, reserved, and very handsome. He loved good music, particularly his eight-track tapes of Isaac Hayes. He loved to host get-togethers and parties at our home. I can remember when I was a little girl, my dad would come home from a long day of work at the corner store he and my uncle owned. After a long day's work, my dad would come home, kick back, and relax. He would sometimes listen to music to unwind. While my dad was in his chill mode, taking the edge off from a long day's work, regardless of how tired he was, my dad would always have room in his space for me. He would allow me to hang out with him, and it seemed no matter what I did, it was okay with him. He allowed me to move around in his space. His fatherly tenderness and attention made me feel loved, wanted, and special. My father's love and acceptance gave me a sense of confidence that I cannot explain and will forever treasure and appreciate. Thank God for the seeds my father planted in my life early on.

When I was seven years of age, my life drastically changed. My father was killed. This abrupt change in my life left me with many questions for God. I was not angry with God. I was confused. I had lots of questions—questions like "How could God take my father from me?" "How was I supposed to get through life without my father?" "Who is going to protect me, guide me, and watch over me?" "Who is going to tell me I am special, beautiful, and loved?" "Who is going to tell me I can do anything and to fear nothing or no one?" My mind was consumed with questions, thoughts, and concerns about my life, my future, and my well-being. Well, God is so amazing, and His grace is totally sufficient.

As I look back on my life and think back to that time, I am reminded of how God had already equipped my life for the changes that were ahead. I am the middle child of three children. I have two brothers, a younger and an older brother. My two brothers became my guardians, my protectors, particularly my older brother. When our father died, my older brother stepped up and stepped into my father's shoes. He was my primary protector. He took this responsibility seriously. Here is a funny story of how serious my older brother took his role as my protector. I can recall a situation that happened when I was in grade school (around third grade). After the death of my father, my mother packed up, and we relocated to another area in the city of New Orleans. We were enrolled in a new school.

At my new school, I recall feeling like the "new girl." I did not know anyone. All the girls had their friends and girl pods. I remember feeling so alone and so left out. All my friends were at my old school far away on the other side of the city. During recess at my new school, I would try to make friends and befriend girls to feel more included. I would ask to join in on games and activities on the playground. There was this boy on the playground, who I guess had noticed I was the new girl and felt like I was going to be his target of bullying. Every game I played, he would come over and play with unnecessary roughness and aggression. One day during recess, I was playing dodgeball with a group of students when this boy, whom I did not know, came over and played with a mean spirit. We were playing dodgeball, and the boy hit the ball with a strong, violent-like stroke and made the ball hit me in the face. I fell to the ground and started crying.

After school, when I arrived home, I told my older brother about the incident. The next day, my brother asked me to point out the boy who had hurt me and made me fall. I pointed the boy out to him. My brother got a good look at the boy. He did not do anything to the boy on that day on the school grounds. My brother told one of my male cousins who was older. My cousin knew of the boy and where the boy lived. He also knew where the boy hung out after school.

One weekend, my brother and cousin were out riding their bikes, and they ran across the boy near my cousin's neighborhood. They cornered him and made the bully boy regret ever harassing me. Let me tell you, I did not have any more trouble out of the boy ever again. Thanks, big brother!

Regardless of whether you grew up feeling special, loved, and protected, it does not negate the fact that you are special, beautiful, and loved. The One who created you specifically and purposely shaped and molded you from love. It is up to you to believe this truth about yourself. It all starts with you. You have the power and ability to reshape, renew, and change your thoughts about yourself. You can accept the truth that you are beautiful, strong, caring, loving, talented, gifted, and special. Or you can choose to believe you are unattractive, unappealing, mentally inept, less than and not good enough. The choice is yours. Whether you choose to believe thoughts of beauty, love, and grace about yourself or self-defeating, self-hating thoughts, you are right. You are what you think.

Today, make a personal commitment to yourself to begin the practice of self-love. Initially, this practice may seem awkward, weird, and uncomfortable. Work through it; you are worth the effort. Write these words on a sheet of paper in large bold letters. Tape the sheet of paper on your bathroom mirror, on your refrigerator, or make the words a screensaver on your cell phone or computer: *I am special. I am beautiful. I am love. I am loved.* Meditate and reflect on these words daily. Ask the Divine for understanding of what these words mean. Allow yourself to be open to receive feedback, inspiration, and renewed understanding of the words. Watch as the words take root in your spirit and blossom in your soul.

My beloved sister, here is what I know to be true: you were created with love by the divine Source that is love. Here is something to get excited about. Here is some good news, and here is the truth. You are beautiful, special, unique, brilliant, kind, caring, fierce, loving, and you are loved. Regardless of what you have been told or what you have been telling yourself up until this point, the truth is, you are wonderful. The One who created you designed you with a special purpose in mind. Everything about you is as it should be. You must make a commitment to yourself today to believe this truth about yourself. The Bible says that as a man or woman thinketh, so is he or she. These words are powerful and loaded with truth. My understanding of this scripture is that what a woman or man thinks of himself or herself is influenced and shaped by the thoughts in his or her mind. If the dominant thoughts in your mind are negative, toxic, and self-defeating, your view of yourself will be distorted and inaccurate. Whereas, on the other hand, if you choose to think and believe you are unique, smart, strong, talented, and gifted, then these thoughts will shape and influence the image in which you view yourself. No one has the power to dictate how you view yourself. No one's words can have power over you without your permission, your acceptance, and your belief in the words. It is the meaning you give the words that give the words power over you. If you choose to give another person such power, it is not the other person who is at fault; you are at fault for giving your power to someone else.

Why would you give another person power to shape and influence your self-image? What insidious thoughts are poisoning your mind and causing you to believe things about yourself that are not true? If you find yourself struggling with this mind-set, here is an opportunity to make a shift in your mind, to consider something new, something different. Ponder this one thought for a second. Look around your life, your family, your community, your city, your state, and even the world; let me know if you can think of another person who is exactly like you. The emphasis is on *exactly* like you. Sure, there are other women with similar features, qualities, challenges, struggles, gifts, abilities, etc., but there is no one in the world exactly like you. Allow this thought to sink in and permeate your consciousness. Allow the thought to linger in your mind until it resonates deep in your spirit. Once you really get it, it will cause a shift in your world. The shift will occur within, and it will have a huge impact on all areas of your life. When the shift occurs in your inner world, it will cause a natural shift in your outer world.

The lens through which you view the world will change. Life will appear more vibrant, more alive and renewed. Once this thought has taken root, it will begin to sprout such wonderful qualities as self-confidence, self-respect, self-love, purpose, joy, and peace. A new you will emerge. Life will have a new and different feel, texture, meaning, excitement, and zest to it. You will begin to look at life totally different. It will appear as though the world around you has changed when, in fact, it will be the changes that have occurred within that will cause the changes without. What a beautiful shift. You will begin to trust yourself more. You will begin to understand your value and your worth. You will begin to question the beliefs that have shaped your life thus far. You will become very curious and consumed with questions—questions about life, about love, about humanity. You will want to know your purpose and your place in the world.

Welcome the questions, and at the same time, breathe and make room for the answers. Allow the answers to flow into your life. Do not try to figure things out or force the answers to come; just surrender and allow the wisdom to flow to you and through you. The answers to your questions will appear in many different forms. When the answers come, you will know and recognize them. A wisdom deep inside you will confirm the answers for you. This wisdom will feel like a quiet whisper, a grounded assurance. This experience will provide a deeper sense of knowing. You will begin to recognize and feel a power that is bigger, greater, and wiser than you moving in your life. You will gradually understand this power is in control. You will understand it is orchestrating every detail of your life.

Just like the morning coming on time every day and the sun setting in the west every evening with no doubt or confusion, you will begin to feel the majesty and awe of this power working in your life. You will begin to understand that your life is special and that you were created for a unique and special purpose that can only be fulfilled by you. This awareness will evoke a strong desire to search for meaning and answers about your life. It will almost become an insatiable hunger, a craving—a hunger and craving to know more about this power, this force that is watching over your life. This Force/Power will begin to stir inside you like a controlled raging fire. The more you discover, the more you will desire to find out more. You will discover that you are a treasure chest filled with so many wonderful gifts, talents, and abilities. Your life will become your own personal adventure. The layers will begin to shed, and the authentic you will start to emerge.

Let me take a moment here to let you know that as your life begins to change/shift, people will change/shift as well. This is a natural process. Surrender and allow the change to happen naturally and organically. When you feel the urge to hold on to people or resist change, just breathe, surrender, accept the moment, and allow it to flow through you. Allow this process to happen in its own way on its own terms. Trust and believe that everything is going to be okay. During this process, there is no need to get alarmed or become fearful. There is no need to fret. You are in good hands. The One who created you is in charge. The best way to get through this process is to *breathe*. Breathe, surrender, and accept things as they are. You are not alone. A higher power is at work. This higher power is with you every step of the way. Even during those uncomfortable moments of change when life seems excruciatingly painful, unbearable, and difficult to endure, take confidence in knowing that your Creator is with you, right by your side.

Initially, the change process will be uncomfortable and painful; however, the pain of letting go is worth the beauty and blessing of finding and discovering your true essence. You will be tempted to hold on to your current life as Spirit is clearing out and making room for your new life and reality. You will question if the journey is worth the effort; you will want to fall back into old patterns and habits.

Your old life is not going to let go without a fight. Circumstances, situations, and events will arise in your life to slough off the dead layers of laziness, fear, and insecurity. These experiences are specifically and divinely designed to strengthen your faith, sharpen your character, and mold your integrity. Think of such moments as your pruning process. In order for a rosebush to produce more beautiful, more fragrant roses, it must be pruned. Old/dead branches must be cut off and removed. This process will arouse and awaken your spirit within, your true self.

It will challenge you and offer you the opportunity to go deeper—to uncover and discover the precious jewels within. My prayer is that you will embrace the moment and surrender to it—surrender to the process; allow the new you to come forth. When you are afraid, ask for courage. When you are feeling lonely and alone, ask Spirit to comfort you; when you are confused, ask for peace and wisdom. As you are going through the process of discovering and uncovering your specialness, your life will change right before your eyes. Many things will appear anew. You will begin to question all relationships in your life. These questions will require courage to answer.

For many of you, this will be your first time exercising your right to choose and take charge of your life. This new reality could evoke strong feelings of anxiety and fear. At times, you may even question or doubt your capacity and wherewithal to deal with the questions that will come up. Let me assure you, you have everything you need within you to walk through this process. So take a deep breath, relax, and trust yourself. Trust yourself and surrender in faith that everything that is being taken away or removed from your life is for your greater good. By removing and letting go of unhealthy/toxic thoughts, situations, friends, etc., you are making room for healthy, meaningful, and quality thoughts, people, and situations to come into your life.

Here's a helpful tip to get you through this season of change and growth. You are going to have to cultivate, nurture, and get comfortable saying the word *no*. I know this will cause a great deal of angst and worry for some of you, but let me assure you, once you begin to understand how valuable your time/life is, you will become more comfortable saying no. The only way to strengthen this boundary is to practice doing it. Get some practice in saying no; start with small situations. The next time you are asked to do something that does not feel good or right to you, just take a deep breath, relax your mind, and simply say no or "No, thank you." Resist the urge to speak after you say no. If you are suddenly gripped with overwhelming anxiety and guilt, here is a strategy to lean on until you are more comfortable saying no: take a quiet, deep breath, count to five, remain quiet, do not say anything, and allow the anxiety to subside and pass through your mind and body. Do not bother to defend or explain your decision. The peace of self-love will melt and dissolve the anxiety. Each time you honor yourself by saying no, you will gain more strength and courage to do it. This is a blessing to both you and the people in your life. If you cannot show up fully and be totally engaged and present with the right heart, spirit, attitude, and intentions, you really are not honoring yourself or the commitment.

Enjoy this phase of discovery; it is rich with so much love, wisdom, and healing. Take time to enjoy the process and watch a new, sexy, strong, confident, caring, creative, beautiful woman blossom right before your eyes. Watch and witness as a sexy goddess claims her position. Once you have discovered your specialness, it will stir up and awaken a sexiness that will radiate from the inside out. I believe sexiness is a state of mind. It is a quality that radiates from within. Being sexy is not in how much you paid for your handbag or how much you spent on your shoes. Sexiness illuminates from your internal value. It is the brilliant sparkle that shines from the many precious jewels in the treasure chest inside you. Being sexy has everything to do with your inner state of being. It is a reflection of what you believe about yourself—mind, heart, and spirit. I believe there are three vital steps to discovering your sexy.

The first step of discovering your sexy is to know that you are loved. This is huge. When a woman feels loved, she feels protected, safe, and secure. She is confident in her own skin. She does not seek approval or validation from others. She has created her own definition of sexy. She is not defined by anyone's limited thoughts, ideas, and beliefs of who they think she is.

The second step of discovering your sexy is full and complete acceptance of who you are, knowing and believing you are enough, and understanding that you are just the person God created you to be. This wisdom is powerful and life changing.

Sexiness is understanding that God did not make a mistake with you. He did not make you less than any other woman. Being sexy is knowing you are a treasure chest of many beautiful qualities and believing God has stored many extraordinary gifts and talents within you.

Sexiness is full and complete acceptance of yourself. This knowingness anchors you in your spirit. During this step, you will begin to understand that you no longer have to hide your shadows and you no longer have to tuck away the parts of yourself that you are ashamed of, embarrassed about, or not pleased with. You can allow the light of love to illuminate those dark areas and set you free. During this phase of discovering your sexy, allow love to dissolve the walls and melt away the fear. Learn to relax and be comfortable in your own skin.

Love has proven itself to you. You are safe. You no longer have to hide from yourself. The walls can come down, and the light of love can shine in and liberate your spirit. During this phase, surrender to the moment, let go of your self-created image, and fully embrace and honor your true self—your true essence. Allow your true essence to radiate from within.

The third step of discovering your sexy is to understand that you are free. God's love for you is your freedom. The One who created you has shaped and formed you in His likeness and His image; therefore, you are love and you are loved. You are not who other people say you are; you are who your Creator says you are. There are no limitations in your life. You have the freedom and privilege to be and become the best person/woman you desire to be or become. With the gift of freedom comes the responsibility of helping other women find their light within and helping them to understand they are free as well. This is sexy love in action—helping other women discover their freedom. Love is freedom, and freedom is a choice. Although the door is open, you have to find the courage within to walk out of your self-created prison. The walls have come down, but you have to decide that you are going to cross over to the other side.

Today, make a conscious decision that you are going to take a leap of faith and start believing that you are special, wonderful, and loved. Take a moment to sit quietly with yourself and reflect on how special you are, then complete the declaration on the next page.

My Declaration

I, _____, promise to love, honor, and cherish myself. I, _____, commit to doing the necessary work to discover my true essence. I, _____, will believe at all times that I am beautiful, special, and wonderful.

Chapter 2

Wake Up, Pay Attention, Ask the Hard Questions

I believe questions are like keys—keys that unlock and open doors to new possibilities and new realities. I believe questions are the fuel that gets the engine of change in motion. When was the last time you stopped and took inventory of your life? Have you taken time to do a mental, spiritual, and emotional temperature check on yourself? Are you awake and present in your life? Where are you in your life right now? Do you even know your current state of existence? Are you living life on your own terms? Are you living with purpose and passion? Or are you stuck inside the continuous/endless loop of tapes and scripts that are playing in your head? Are you living in the past, wasting precious time thinking about people, things, or situations that are dead, irrelevant, and unimportant? Are you in charge of your life? Are you taking responsibility for your choices and decisions? Are you allowing other people to dictate and determine your quality of life, your happiness, your joy, and your peace? Whom have you given your power to? If you have answered yes to some of these questions or if you do not know the answer to these questions, the big question is *why*?

Many people are walking around asleep, numb, or on autopilot in their lives. How is your current state of existence serving you? What thoughts are dominating your mind? Are you living in a positive state of love, peace, joy, and happiness? If not, who do you think is responsible for your current state and your quality of life? Who do you think has to give account for the choices and decisions in your life? Here's a clue: you do. Why do you think someone else knows what is better for you than you know for yourself? Do you not trust yourself—your own inner wisdom? Do you not trust yourself to make wise, sensible, and smart decisions? Are you not courageous enough to move from the sideline and get in the game called your life? Are you not willing to take healthy risks and stretch yourself to discover your potential, to become a better person, to experience a higher quality of life? Where did you lose yourself? How did you get here? Are you comfortable in this place? Do you want to change? Do you desire a different reality? If so, what changes are you willing to make? What are you going to do differently that will yield a better quality of life? Whose responsibility do you think it is to change your life? What are you going to do about *your* life? What are you waiting on? Whom are you waiting for to come rescue you from your self-created prison? How much longer are you going to sit there and blame other people for your current state, situation, and predicament? When are you going to take responsibility for where you are and reclaim your power? When are you going to get up and get on with your life? Who do you think is coming to save you? How long are you going to sit there

You Are Enough

and whine, complain, mope, and wallow in your self-pity? Get your ass up!

Today is a great day for a fresh start, a new beginning. Now is a good time to make *you* your first and main priority. Here is your moment to rise from the ashes, dust yourself off, and get on with the business of living your life. This moment is rich with so many possibilities. This moment is a gift that has been given to you—an opportunity to start over, to begin anew, and to create a new reality.

Take out your journal or grab a notebook. Imagine this day as a blank canvas that has been placed before you—a blank canvas with no borders or boundaries, a blank canvas of unlimited possibilities. On this canvas you are free to color outside the lines. You have the freedom to pick any and all the colors you would like. You are free to draw in any direction that feels good to you. You are allowed to make broad strokes, big shapes, and interesting and unique figures, and you have permission to do whatever you would like.

Feel free to create the life you desire to live. Go for it! Accept the precious gift that is wrapped in this moment. Allow your spirit to speak to you. Ask for what you want. Feel free to create your ideal reality. Allow your spirit to breathe, move, and create. Ponder and contemplate the type of life you desire. Do not put any restrictions or limitations on your desire. Allow your spirit to freely roam and have full expression. Imagine you are a little girl in your playroom with a big, wide canvas in front of you. What kind of life would you create? Give yourself time and space to ponder these questions. Allow your spirit to be free. Feel the aliveness of Spirit surging through you as you are pondering your ideal life. Feel the thrill and excitement of creativity coursing through your body.

While your journal or notebook is still open, write down what is flowing through you. If this is your first time creating, visualizing, or imagining a new life, be prepared; a strong surge of ideas may flow through you, and it may be difficult to jot everything down. Be patient, sit as long as you can, and try to capture as much as possible. This wellspring has been waiting to be released inside you. The force of the energy flowing through you is a sign that thoughts, dreams, and ideas have been lying dormant in your spirit for many years. The release is long overdue. The Power that is at work inside you is giving birth to your new reality and making room for fresh new possibilities to emerge in your spirit. Do not try to judge or understand anything; just write as the thoughts, ideas, and possibilities flow through you. Allow your spirit to create and have full expression. After this process, sit quietly and allow Spirit to speak to you, guide you, and reveal awesome, magical, and beautiful things to you. Ask Spirit to speak to you, to show you the way, to help you understand what is meaningful and true in your life.

What if someone told you that this life is the only life you're going to get? What if you were informed that this life you're living is the real deal, not a dress rehearsal or a warm-up? What if you were told that when the clock strikes the final hour, you will not have the option for a do-over or repeat? What if you truly understood that your physical form is not going to last forever? How would that impact your choices and decisions? What if you could grasp that your physical form has an expiration date? What if you understood this is your life and it is happening right here, right now? How would these questions impact your thoughts, decisions, actions, and relationships? Would this reality inspire you to wake up, be present, and start living with purpose and passion? Would it paralyze you with fear because you would look back with regret at all the time you have wasted, relationships you have not nurtured, moments you did not act upon, decisions you failed to make, or even more sadly, faith you did not have in yourself? Well, today is a new day in your life, an opportunity for a new beginning. Allow the words I am about to share with you to encourage, inspire, and motivate you.

If you are reading this book, you still have time; there is hope for you. You still have time to do something meaningful and productive with your life. You still have time to make out your list of dreams, goals, and desires. You still have time to learn how to foster healthy relationships. You still have time to tell the people in your life that you love them and appreciate all the wonderful things they bring into your life. If you need some momentum to get you going or some encouragement to help you get moving in a positive direction, think back to a time in your life when you were faced with a very difficult situation and you had to find the courage within to make a tough decision and step out on faith. Think about how things begin to fall in place once you made the commitment to change your situation or state. I am not saying it was easy or without difficulty to change whatever situation you were facing then. I am saying you found the strength and courage to change your situation then, so I believe you have what it takes to change your life now.

Awaken the courage within that is lying dormant awaiting an opportunity to show its strength and power. During this season, give yourself permission to express your true feelings. Be okay with crying; your tears will strengthen and heal you. Your tears will clear your mind, cleanse your heart, and provide clarity for what lies ahead of you. Your tears will clear the fog and allow you to see things more accurately. When situations and challenges show up in your life to develop your faith muscle, stay the course, feel the discomfort, and press through the moment; it will pass. If you can endure these circumstances, you will build a strong, resilient character.

As I look back on my life, I am so thankful for the many tears, heartaches, disappointments, and seeming setbacks. Those experiences were part of shaping and forming my character and giving substance to my life story—a story I hope will provide hope, healing, and inspiration to every person who reads this book. As far back as I can remember, I have always had a loaded arsenal of questions about life, about God, and about my existence. I remember when I was a young girl, every summer my mother would pack our bags and send my brothers and me to spend the entire summer with our grandmother in Mississippi. Back then, when I was a little girl and when my grandmother was a younger woman, she was hardworking and no-nonsense. My grandmother believed in working hard, living right, helping others, and going to church every Sunday. There must be something to glean from my grandmother's values and her wisdom.

My grandmother is still alive. She is eighty-six years old and still going strong. She is grounded, tender, wise, and so beautiful. She is a devout Christian. My grandmother knows the Lord. She is a praying woman. My grandma can get a prayer through to Jesus. As a matter of fact, I believe my grandmother has Jesus's personal cell number, and I believe she is in His faves list of people, meaning when my grandmother calls on Jesus, He always answers her prayers.

My grandmother bought me my first Bible. When I was a little girl, she would read Bible stories to me and my younger brother. Thanks to my grandmother, I have always had a sense of God. She instilled Christian principles and values in me as a little girl. I am grateful for my grandmother, and the many blessings she has imparted in my life.

During our summer visits in Mississippi with my grandmother, she would take us to church every Sunday. Her denomination is COGIC, which stands for Church of

God in Christ. At my grandmother's church, it seemed we stayed in church all day. The preacher was an older man, very kind; all the church members loved, adored, and respected him. My grandmother always made sure we were polite and respectful toward the pastor. If, for some reason, we forgot to be polite or were not paying attention, she would give us the "you are in big trouble when we get to the car" look, which provoked us to be nice and kind to the pastor at all times because none of us wanted Grandma to deal with us once we got to the car after church service.

My grandmother is a good Christian woman, and she loves the Lord. But back when we were kids, she had no problem grabbing a switch from any bush and making us call on Jesus. During the church service, as the preacher was delivering his Sunday sermon, in my spirit, the teachings of the preacher did not make sense to me. I found myself having a different reaction from other members in the congregation to the preacher's sermon. It seemed as though I were hearing a different message from the message the other parishioners were hearing. I could not understand what people were falling out, shouting, and screaming about. I could barely understand the message, and my goodness, the meaning was difficult to grasp due to all the "whooping and hollering" done by the pastor. I was confused. Even as a young girl in my limited understanding of God then, I remember having very different views about God from what the pastor preached on Sundays. According to the preacher, God was presented as some type of all-powerful, controlling taskmaster who would punish or curse his followers if they did not go to church every Sunday. I struggled with this idea. I thought to myself, *Wow. Really? Who wants to be in that type of relationship?* The pastor's teachings created disturbing images and puzzling thoughts in my mind and spirit. There were so many contradictions in my mind. As I mentioned earlier, my grandmother would read Bible stories to us when we were kids. In one of the Bible stories she read to us, it stated that God is love (1 John 4:8). Now, if God is love, then the controlling-taskmaster view that the pastor preached could not be accurate because love is not controlling. It was such contradictions that raised so many questions in my mind and in my spirit about God, life, and the true essence of God's love for us. As a little girl sitting there listening to the pastor's teachings about God and what is required to be loved by Him, I thought to myself, *There is no hope for me. I will never make it on God's list. God will never love me.* I am a hopeless case because back home in New Orleans, we did not attend church every Sunday. We only went to church when my mother was rested and felt like going. My summers in Mississippi with my grandmother were the most I had ever gone to church. To say the least, these opposing thoughts and beliefs caused great internal conflict. My view of God did not align with the preacher's teachings. I did not try to prove the preacher wrong; I simply made a quiet petition in my heart to know and experience God for myself in a way that would allow God to be real and true for me. So that's how my journey to experience God began.

I did not want to die, go to heaven, and then meet God. I wanted to know and experience God in my life right here, right now on earth. I strongly desired to experience heaven on earth! I wanted to *know* God, get up close and personal with Him, ask questions, seek knowledge, and allow God's wisdom to speak to me from within and throughout my life.

I am a very rational person. So I needed to experience God for myself. I am the type of person whom you cannot tell something to and expect to believe it just because you said it. Well, let me clarify my comment. My grandmother is probably the only person who can tell me something and I will believe whatever she tells me without asking any questions. The wisdom in her eyes has an assurance that confirms she is telling me the truth. Because I am a rational person, I must be able to test ideas, concepts, and notions and experience these things for myself, and then I will know such things to be true. Therefore, I needed to test and experience God for myself in order for me to know God to be true. Just like with any relationship, you have to get up close and personal/intimate with a person in order to really and truly know him/her. Many moons ago (I guess around age seventeen), that is exactly what I set out to do. I ventured out on a quest to get to know God/my Creator for myself. This experience was important to me. I did not seek advice or approval from anybody. This was a personal choice, and no one was going to stop me. It was an absolute must that I experience God for myself. Otherwise, God would seem like one of those mythical characters such as the Easter Bunny, the Tooth Fairy, or Santa Claus. I needed to experience God/Spirit in a way that would let me know He is real.

My curiosity and desire to get to know and understand the One who gave me this gift called life and my desire to get to know myself in a deeper, more intimate way have led me down some interesting, lonely dark roads in my life; I have spent my share of days in the wilderness on my journey to my promised land. Every step along my journey has revealed new truths and new realities about God. When I was a little girl, I thought the Bible stories my grandmother read to me were fascinating and very interesting. I had no idea the stories were parables—stories of real-life experiences. Wow! Life truly is an exciting, mysterious, and wonderful journey of discovery.

I have experienced many Bible verses unfold in my life. I have experienced Bible verses play out in my life to the point where I said to myself, *OMG! Let's take a closer look*. For example, such Bible scriptures as "Weeping may endure for a night, but joy cometh in the morning" (Psalm 30:5), "God is able" (2 Corinthians 9:8), and "I will *never* leave you nor forsake you" (Joshua 1:5). Now, this scripture "I will *never* leave you nor forsake you" is loaded. This is an interesting word choice: *never!* Did God really intend to use the word *never*? I mean, other words and phrases were available, like "most of the time," "in many situations," "on most days," or "during some situations." But no, God chose the word *never*. My goodness, that makes me happy and gives me great comfort and reassurance! To me, this scripture means that no matter where I find myself in life and regardless of the situation or circumstances, God is *always* there.

My excitement about Bible verses coming to life continues with this passage, "God is able to do exceedingly abundantly above *all* we can ask or think, according to the power that works in us." Okay, this scripture really tickles my fancy because I have a very active imagination. I believe anything is possible. So the fact that God included this passage in the Bible and purposely chose the words *exceedingly, abundantly*, and *above all*, my goodness, this fills my heart with so much joy and excitement until my cup runneth over.

With each new revelation, it created a deeper yearning and hunger for more truth, more love, more understanding, more growth, and more learning. I wanted to know more about God. I was fascinated by this Ultimate Being, this Source. I longed to know more about Him. I craved more wisdom and understanding.

My desire to learn more about God led me to enroll in a disciple course at a church near my home. The course was designed to teach seekers/students about the Bible and about God. The disciple course included four phases. Each phase of the course required a serious commitment of thirty to forty minutes of daily reading and note taking, reflecting and praying six days a week, and participation in a two-and-a-half-hour weekly group meeting for thirty-four weeks for each phase of the four-part course. I was eager. I was hungry. I was willing to make the commitment. I was an avid student. I arrived on time for every group meeting. I asked lots of questions during our classroom sessions. I was totally enthralled and intrigued by this Power/Force called God, Jesus, and the Holy Spirit. Upon completing each phase of the course, I was peaked and ready to learn more. The disciple course was a wonderful experience. If I had to summarize what I learned about the Bible, about God, it is that the Bible is a book about love. The Bible is an interesting and enchanting story about the One who created us and His desire to take us on a magical and exciting journey of self-discovery and love actualized.

I learned God/Spirit only wants what is best for us because God/Spirit is love. How sexy of God to give us such a wonderful and magical gift called life! This discovery/unveiling has turned my life into a more exciting adventure. It is like waking up and experiencing Christmas every day. I wake up in the morning peaked with curiosity and excitement. I am so grateful for each day's supply of daily bread. God is awesome. I feel like a kid who has a best friend with magical superpowers.

Every day is so exciting; it is filled with mystery and love. I wake up every morning with anticipation and excitement in my heart. My life is grand. Since I was a young girl, I have always been very curious about life, living, and discovering potential (mine as well as other people's potential). Since my awareness of God has become more intimate, my curiosity about life has been turned up ten thousand notches. I feel as though I have been plugged into an electrical current—an electrical current that is so powerful yet so tender and gentle.

A shift has occurred in my life. I feel as though I have stepped into a new place. I don't have the exact words to describe it; however, the feeling is very real. I am so grateful for the experiences that have come into my life to wake me up, get my attention, and challenge me to ask the hard questions. As a result, I have discovered a peace within that surpasses all understanding, a calmness that keeps me grounded, a love that is ever present, and a hope that grows with each new day. It feels as though a floodgate has opened up inside me. My spirit is like a wellspring of amazing discoveries. This is very exciting.

Take a moment to sit quietly with yourself and reflect on where you are in your life right now; decide on the quality of life you desire, then complete the declaration on the next page.

My Declaration

I, _____, promise to wake up, get present, and ask the hard questions. I, _____, commit to discovering my potential. I, _____, believe I have the power to change my current state and create the life I desire.

Chapter 3

I Am Not Your Opinion of Me

Many women waste their time defining themselves through the eyes of others. They are looking for answers to questions that must come from within. They are seeking acceptance and approval from individuals who do not have the power or insight to give them such information. Insight comes from the Source that created us. Power resides on the inside and exudes from the inside out. It is so unfortunate and, at the same time, very ironic that it takes strength and courage to be your own person when I believe that is our main purpose in life. I believe we were created to discover who we are. Yet people will attack, judge, ridicule, and attempt to sabotage people who are about the business of discovering their true essence.

I find it very interesting that people are comfortable offering unsolicited opinions and advice about who they think you are or who they think you should be. I mean, how can another person tell you who they think you should be? How do they know? They did not create you. How do they know the depth and scope of your many capacities? What gives them the right to tell you who you are? What gives another person the audacity to tell you who they think you can be or become? This is comical. When such people feel the need to share their unsolicited advice and opinions, I simply erect an iron wall in my mind and spirit. I don't allow their words to penetrate my personal space. I look at the person in utter amusement. I laugh and say to myself, "This person in front of me is such an idiot." In my mind, before I walk away, I am thinking to myself, *Stop talking to me.*

I have very low tolerance for nonsense; I politely excuse myself from the environment of people who have negative thoughts and opinions. I do not allow their poisonous words to infiltrate my sacred soil—my mind and spirit.

When I take a moment to ponder why someone would feel inclined or compelled to inject negative comments and opinions into another person's life, I think it has a lot to do with the person's lack of self-awareness and self-respect. I believe people who spew negative words like venom are miserable and unhappy in their lives. I believe such individuals have not discovered their own essence. I believe it is important to set healthy boundaries in your life. People have the right to say whatever they'd like to say; however, I have a duty and responsibility to protect my mental, spiritual, and emotional well-being and to guard my mind and spirit from such negative people and influences. I do not give other people the power or privilege to dictate or control my life. I respect other people's point of view; however, I do not allow another person's opinion to control my life or how I view myself. I am a caring, considerate, and kind human being, but I am not a nice person. Nice people are like doormats; they do not fully understand their value and worth. They allow people to walk all over them and waste their time, and they allow people to treat them with little or no dignity and respect. Nice people usually are discarded and dismissed when they no longer serve a purpose or meet the needs of a negative, dysfunctional person. Nice people do not have healthy boundaries in their relationships. They allow people to influence and manipulate their thoughts and emotions. Nice people say yes when no is the best answer. They fear rejection, and they waste enormous amounts of time and energy worrying about what other people think of them.

My question is, why? Why waste your time and energy on people who do not respect you? Why keep company with people who have self-serving motives? Why give a damn about people who have no respect or regard for your precious time and energy?

After reading this book, I hope you will find the courage within to stand up for yourself, set healthy boundaries in your relationships, and kill the desire to please people. I hope you will release all toxic, self-sabotaging thoughts from your mind. My desire is that you will release all self-defeating thoughts that are telling you to keep unhealthy people in your life. My hope is that you will set yourself free by making better choices and decisions in your life. This one shift in your life could produce huge changes in other areas of your life.

Today, make a declaration to yourself that you will get rid of toxic people in your life and set healthy boundaries in your friendships and relationships. When you set these boundaries, be prepared for a backlash of anger and resentment from toxic people. Once you make a commitment to love and respect yourself, you are no longer a host for them to feed upon; therefore, they may become angry or bitter with you because now they must seek and find another negative host to feast upon. Also, when you make this change in your life, some people will think of you as mean, tough, and firm.

As of today, you are okay with what people think about you because you are no longer defined by other people's opinion of you. You are no longer allowing another person's opinion to control your life. The next time someone is compelled to share their unwelcomed advice with you, guard your mind and spirit.

Remember, you were uniquely and wonderfully created for a special purpose. God has plans for your life. People have the right to think and say whatever they'd like, and you have every right not to be disturbed by their thoughts or opinions. People who truly know you—people who know your character and the qualities that make you the woman that you are—will not be fazed by your decision to set healthy boundaries in your life because they already respect your boundaries. Value your life and guard your personal space. Your life is special and scared. Be mindful of who and what you give your energy and attention to.

Today, I encourage you to find the courage and strength within to be your own person, your own woman. Put safeguards around your life. If you are reading this book and you have come to realize that you have not set healthy boundaries in your life and as a result you are stuck in your life, confused about who you are, and you have no clue how special and wonderful you are, then today is a great day to begin doing the work—to start digging to uncover why you are where you are in your life.

At some point along your journey, you lost your way. For years, you have been believing stories about yourself that are not true. You have been believing lies and stories that have led you to this juncture, this book, this crossroads in your life. It is amazing how words can have so much power and influence over our thoughts and decisions. People can be so cruel and hurtful with their words. They can say things that totally crush your spirit and cause you to create illusions about yourself. Many women today have defined themselves based on the unkind and hurtful words people have spoken into their lives. They are living out the lies people have spoken about them, and they have allowed the lies to become truths for them.

So many women are walking around playing these tapes—these stories over and over in their head—and totally believing these lies. They have lost sight of who they truly are. They are believing things that are not true; therefore, they are living below their potential. You do not have to remain in this state. You have the power to renew your mind and change your current situation. You can dispel the lies, and you can begin your journey of seeking the truth about who you are.

Today, make a commitment to yourself that you are no longer going to believe the lies other people have told you. You are going to stop the repetitive loop of tapes and scripts that has been playing in your mind. Today, make a commitment to yourself to cast down all negative, toxic, and self-defeating thoughts. Decide today, you are going to ask God to show you who you are and how special you are. You can begin the healing process by taking inventory of your current mental, spiritual, and emotional state. It is important that you are totally honest and transparent with yourself during this process. Become keenly aware of the scripts and stories that are playing in your head at this moment. Focus all your attention on the thoughts that are in your mind right now. Pay close attention to the thoughts. Do not judge what is playing in your mind. Simply take notice of your thoughts; put your inner attention on the thoughts. Now that you are paying attention, when a thought arises in your mind, ask yourself these three questions: Is this true? Is this thought a fact? Is this who I am? Once you have asked these questions, sit quietly, allow your mind to slow down, and become still so you can hear the truth. Allow the truth to clear the fog, release your spirit, and show you who you truly are. By putting your attention on your thoughts, you are breaking the loop and destroying the yoke or the cycle of the thought. This is the beginning of a breakthrough, a step toward healing.

Now that you have become aware of your thoughts, it is time to go deeper to uncover and discover the source, the root of your thoughts. It is time to make the shift inward. It is time to go within to discover your true self. Making the shift inward may cause some anxiety. You may feel the urge to distract yourself with something or someone. If or when this urge arises, pay attention to your thoughts and focus on your desire for healing and wholeness. Begin your journey of discovery by setting aside thirty minutes daily, either first thing in the morning before you start your day or before you go to bed at night. This time of meditation is your time to listen to God and your spirit.

Initially, it may seem somewhat difficult or uncomfortable to sit alone in silence. You may notice an ongoing string of thoughts in your mind, you may experience a strong urge to get up, or you may notice a low current of anxiety coursing through your body. Relax and be patient with yourself. This is totally normal. Because meditation is a new and unfamiliar experience, your mind and body are trying to figure out what is going on. Your mind and body will do one of two things: resist or adapt to the change. During your first attempt to meditate, you may only be able to sit for five minutes. This is okay; applaud yourself for having the courage to make the effort.

The next time you attempt to meditate, you may feel comfortable sitting for fifteen minutes, and the next time, twenty minutes. With each effort to meditate, you will notice a decrease in the mental noise. You will become more aware of your thoughts. The continuous loop of mental chatter will slowly lose its momentum. Do not try to force the process. Eventually, the noise will go quiet, and stillness will arise. During this process, take long, deep breaths and allow Spirit to usher you into the quiet place within. It is important that you are patient with yourself. Keep in mind these negative thoughts have been playing in your mind for years; they have somewhat become embedded in your mind. It will require lots of love, patience, and kindness to destroy the current cycle and create a new one. Also, be mindful of the ego's attempt to get you to give up on yourself. Your ego will tell you that meditation is a waste of time and that nothing good or positive is going to happen for you. When such thoughts arise in your mind, just breathe and release them.

Meditation is powerful. It is healing, revealing, and transforming. The goal of meditation is to get up close and personal with yourself—to learn how to be comfortable in your own skin. During your quiet moments of meditation, ask God to speak to you. Ask God to show you who you are, why you are here, and the purpose for your life. Sit in silence and listen for the quiet whisper of God to speak to you. Let the healing begin. It is your birthright to have full self-expression. God created you for a special purpose.

Here is a secret that I hope will set you free and destroy the stronghold of fear and doubt off your mind and your life. No one is greater or more special than anyone else. We are all the same. The same God who shaped and formed your being is the same God who gave shape and form to my life. Isn't this beautiful? Doesn't this thought make you feel special and loved? Now that you have begun the healing process, you are well on your way to a new reality. I am so excited for you. You have the power to totally transform your life into something wonderful and magical. Isn't it exciting to know you have the option to shift and move your life in a different direction? You no longer have to wait for someone to give you permission to live your life on your own terms. The power to create the life you desire is in this moment; the power is in your hands. The thought of creating the life you desire should make you feel so excited to be in this moment regardless of your current circumstances.

There is so much power in this present moment. If you will accept the invitation to heal, the course of your entire life will change for the better. By saying yes to the invitation, you are saying yes to a better, brighter, and more fulfilling life. Now is a good time to accept the invitation and begin the journey of creating the life you desire. Tomorrow is not promised, and yesterday is dead and in the past. Knowing and sensing that the present moment is filled with so much hope and promise should make you feel strong and confident. To firmly believe you have the power to change your life should tickle your fancy and excite your soul. You are no longer controlled by other people's opinion. You are free—free to choose and free to be who you are.

As I look back on my life, I am grateful for every situation and circumstance I have experienced in my life. I have come to know that God's grace is sufficient. No matter how hurtful, painful, or difficult the situation appeared, once the dust settled and the smoke cleared, I could always look back and see where God's hand of grace was covering me, leading me, guiding me, and walking me through every situation. I can look back and see how God was breaking me, shaping me, molding me, and preparing me for the next phase of my journey. I believe there is a blessing in every heartbreak if you will allow God to use the pain in His own way.

I have never been the type of person to hold grudges or not allow forgiveness to cleanse the waters within. Forgiving someone, accepting the situation, releasing the emotions, and moving on with my life have played a huge role in how my life is so wonderful and awesome today. I feel sorry for people who allow dead issues of the past to control their lives. Forgiveness is so powerful. It allows you to set yourself free and release your spirit from the bondage of anger, hate, and fear. Forgiveness is not so much about the other person as it is about you; however, forgiveness does have the power to heal both the victim and the perpetrator because it allows love to flow in, and love begins to heal the wound. By allowing forgiveness to enter the equation of hurt plus pain, it offers the opportunity to yield a different outcome. Instead of holding on to bitter, unresolved anger and disappointment, when you add forgiveness to the equation, it opens the wound, and it allows the pain and hurt to be released from the situation.

Forgiveness offers the opportunity for healing and restoration. Forgiveness is rooted in love, and love opens the door for healing. Forgiveness creates the opportunity for both hearts to be healed. Forgiveness can restore the integrity of relationships and allow a new dynamic to form in the relationship. Forgiveness opens the door for healing to enter. It is the place where you can release your hurt and pain. Forgiveness allows you to unravel the entanglements in your spirit—entanglements such as hate, bitterness, resentment, and lack of trust—entanglements that have caused you to be stuck and spinning in the same loop of pain.

Forgiveness breaks the cycle of anger, and it destroys the yoke of the pain. Forgiveness is like a healing elixir that soothes, calms, and restores you back to love, back to life, back to living.

If there is someone in your life that you need to forgive, do it today. Set yourself free today. Forgiveness is a choice. Forgiveness is freedom—freedom to move forward in your life. Choose forgiveness and freedom today. The choice is yours. Remember, you are no longer defined by other people's opinion of you. Take a moment to sit quietly with yourself and reflect on what thoughts, ideas, and opinions are not serving you well; decide to release those thoughts and renew your mind, then complete the declaration on the next page.

My Declaration

I, _____, promise to set myself free from other people's opinion of me. I, _____, commit to discovering the power within. I, _____, believe I have the power to change my current state and create the life I desire.

Chapter 4

Dream Big / Burn the Boat / Have Faith

Have you ever taken time to ponder why some people's dreams come true and others do not? Have you thought about what makes those individuals different from the people whose dreams are never fulfilled or realized? Do you think it is because some people are more gifted and talented than others? Do you think "dream realizers" have a special edge or advantage over you and other people? Or are you contemplating the notion that you have received an unfair advantage in life and you are less capable than those who have achieved their dreams? Regardless of the nonsense you have been told or the nonsense you are telling yourself right now, I am here to tell you that all of it is garbage; it is not true. We are all the same. Our Creator created us equally. I believe dreams are given to each of us. I believe dreams are placed inside every human being—dreams that inspire us to stretch into our potential. I believe dreams are like a call or an invitation into the unknown. Dreams are like a candle in our heart that lights the way toward our destiny, our purpose in life. Dreams are powerful. Dreams are transforming. Dreams can give a hopeless person inspiration, motivation, and determination to rise above his or her current situation. I love to take time on Sunday afternoons to ponder and reflect—reflect on my life and give thanks for the many dreams I have witnessed come to pass in my life.

I love to swim in the ocean of possibilities in my mind. I enjoy thinking of what could be—a new dream coming into existence. I love to sit back, relax, and allow my spirit to freely roam and discover new territories and new possibilities.

As far back as I can remember, even as a young girl, I have always had an active imagination. I have always had an insatiate mental playground where I would dream and ponder possibilities. I have always had a healthy curiosity about life, love, relationships, success, happiness, and joy. I also have a strong desire to know and to better understand the differentiating factor between what makes dreams come true and the reason or reasons why dreams do not come true.

When I look back on my life at the many dreams I have seen come to pass in my life, I am in awe and amazement at the Spirit/Power that allows us to conceive and manifest things from the unseen realm into the physical realm. I am in total awe of this power, this force, and this vast, limitless, boundless capacity within us that allows things to manifest into our physical existence. This is very intriguing and fascinating to me.

I believe the most important factor that makes a huge difference between dreams being realized and dreams not being realized is faith. I firmly believe when we dare to act in faith, it evokes a power within us that is greater, bigger, and more intelligent than our physical and mental capacity. I purposely used the words "act in faith" because

I believe faith without works is wishful thinking. To act in faith means to act with the confidence and assurance that the unmanifested will manifest itself into your physical reality. In other words, to act in faith means to believe that what is conceived in the spiritual world will come to pass in the physical world. I can recall an experience in my life when I was a teenager and I witnessed, firsthand, the power of faith in action. I witnessed the potency of believing in the possibility of what could be. When I turned sixteen years old, I got my first job. I worked at McDonald's as a cashier/fry girl. I worked part-time in the evenings after school, on weekends, and on holidays. I wanted to work so I could earn my own money, buy my own clothes, and have my own coins to put in my purse.

While working at McDonald's in high school, the management team thought I was a reliable and dedicated employee. They offered to put me through the management training program. They were prepared to groom me for a long-term career as a McDonald's employee. Initially, I was honored and pleased they saw such potential in me. However, I was not interested in becoming a long-term employee. I was not interested in working at McDonald's for the next twenty-plus years (let me say here that there is nothing wrong with having this as a career aspiration). I had no desire to explore this option. In my small town of Liberty, Mississippi, there were limited resources to explore career opportunities. In spite of this reality, I was certain I was not going to pursue a career at McDonald's.

In my small town, after high school, most girls either pursued a career at McDonald's, got a job at the poultry plant, joined the military, or attended the local junior college. None of these options appealed to me. I wanted more out of life. I wanted to explore some of the dreams and possibilities my brother and I had dreamed about when we were younger.

I have always believed that an education is important and that it is the one thing no one can take from you. I enjoy learning. I maintained an honor roll status throughout my high school years. In spite of my environment and limited resources that were available, I was not willing to settle for working at McDonald's, working at the poultry plant, joining the military, or enrolling at the local junior college. I wanted to pursue a higher education. I wanted to earn a four-year college degree from a university. I should mention here that no one in my mother's or father's family had graduated with a four-year degree from a college or university. My mother has a high school education. My father was a member of the US Marine Corp. After his military career, my father attended a junior college. I had limited knowledge of and support for how to choose a good college and how to submit an admissions application. I was totally clueless about the number of credits required to earn a degree. In spite of the many questions and the many unknowns, I was willing. I was willing to act in faith and give it a try. Let me tell you, this is truly faith in action.

I did not have answers to many of the questions that were looming in my mind; however, I was certain I did not want to stay in my small town in Mississippi and work at McDonald's; nothing about that life appealed to me.

Here's how God is so awesome. One weekend, my boyfriend at the time asked me to go with him to visit his older cousin at Southern University and A&M College in Baton Rouge, Louisiana. I said yes to the invitation.

When we arrived on the campus, I was totally mesmerized by the people, the atmosphere, and the collegiate feeling in the air. The students seemed so sharp, sophisticated, and mature. When I saw the students, I silently whispered to myself in my spirit, "This is where I am going to earn my college degree." The experience presented an opportunity in my life that I am not sure would have happened otherwise (thank you, DTH, for this experience). It changed the course of my life. When I returned home from my visit to Southern University and A&M College, I was peaked with hope and excitement. That night, I could hardly sleep. I lay awake thinking and imagining myself walking around on the campus dressed like the students I had seen on the campus. I imagined myself looking sharp, sophisticated, and mature just like them. These thoughts consumed me. Every day and night, I thought about what my life would be like as a student at Southern University and A&M College.

Meanwhile, back in the real world, I did not know what was required to get accepted into the university. I did not know how to complete the admissions packet. I did not know how I was going to pay for tuition and out-of-state fees. At that time, all I knew was that I had made up my mind that I was going to pursue my college education at Southern University and A&M College. There is something powerful about a made-up mind and a determined spirit. Looking back, I don't know how I completed all the complicated admissions paperwork. My mother did not have time to help me with the admissions paperwork. She was a single parent who was busy working to put food on the table for her three children. I had no one to turn to for support and guidance. I believe the hand of God was guiding me through the process. I believe when we take one step of faith, God takes ten big steps for us. This is faith in action. So line by line, I read each question and provided information to the best of my knowledge. I mailed the packet, said a prayer, crossed my fingers, and hoped for an acceptance letter. It seemed like a thousand years between mailing my admissions packet and waiting for an answer. When I received the letter from Southern University and A&M College in the mail, I was gripped with anxiety and excitement at the same time. I thought to myself, *What if I did not get accepted? Would I have to go back to McDonald's, ask for my job back, and ask to be reconsidered for the management training program? Or perhaps, if it was an acceptance letter, my life would change for the better.* When I opened the letter and read that I had been accepted into the school, I was overwhelmed with feelings of shock, awe, and gratitude. This was the beginning of a new reality for me. This new opportunity would open my life up to many possibilities. Faith coupled with intense, unyielding belief in the impossible can change your life.

As I look back on things now, I believe it was my faith in God that gave me the wisdom and courage to get through the difficult task of completing all the necessary paperwork and submitting the proper documentation.

When I left home at the age of eighteen headed to college, I did know how things were going to work out, but in a strange way, I was confident that the One who brought me this far would be with me and see me through to the other side. Even with all the questions and doubts as I began my college experience, I kept a spirit of faith. I kept the light of hope burning within me. I figured if I could find the courage within to show up, then that step of faith would build momentum to get me to graduation. It was not an easy journey; however, it was a great learning experience. I learned so much about myself. With every obstacle and every challenge, I became stronger, smarter, wiser, and better. The mission was accomplished. My dream came true. I am proud to say I am a graduate of Southern University and A&M College. Not only that, I am a first-generation college graduate in my family. This is a new legacy for our family.

Now, my nieces and nephews have a road map to follow. I have instilled in them that pursuing a college education is a viable option for them. Today, my nephew is enrolled at Alcorn State University. I am so proud of him. I believe there is something powerful about a made-up mind and a determined spirit. I believe that with God, anything is possible.

After my dream of earning a college degree came true, I was inspired to go after other dreams. I believe the bigger the dream, the bigger the mountains and obstacles. I have learned that mountains and obstacles are not always bad things. I believe certain challenges are purposely designed to bring out our potential. I believe during the "dream birthing" process, new skills are discovered—new skills such as perseverance, patience, focus, resilience, character, courage, hope, and most importantly, faith. There have been many moments in my life when mountains and obstacles have seemed too big to surmount.

While pursuing some of my dreams, I have been in situations where life has put the squeeze on me and almost made me say uncle. The pressure was so overwhelming; it almost made me give up and go back home to the nest, to my safe place. There have been times when life became very difficult to manage. A sense of defeat attempted to shroud my spirit and discourage me from reaching higher and pursuing my dreams. There have been times when it was very hard to press forward. I have had moments where giving up felt like the best option; however, the spirit of determination that dwells within all of us would not let me to give up on myself. Each time I felt weak, weary, and worn, I would cry out and ask God for wisdom, strength, and guidance. This act of crying out to God awakened a renewed strength within me and gave me a second wind to carry on. My renewed strength gave me the courage to hang in there, to see it through, to tough it out, and to press forward. I have discovered that the bigger the dream, more is required of you. Now that I have experienced many of my dreams come to pass, I understand this concept a little better; however, when I am in the midst of giving birth to a dream, most times, I feel as though I have bitten off more than I could chew. I sometimes feel as though I do not have the capacity within to give birth to the dream.

With each climb higher toward bigger dreams and goals, I have discovered and learned new things about myself. I have discovered there is a power source within all of us that is available to us at any given moment. With each climb, each dream realized, I have developed more wisdom, more patience, more toughness, more confidence, more peace, and more serenity. During the rough and tough moments of the climb toward a new dream, during the darkest nights when it seemed daylight was not going to come—those times when it seemed my heart would not stop aching or those moments when it seemed my light of hope was going dim—God was there. There is a Bible verse that says weeping may endure for a night but joy comes in the morning. I have discovered for myself that these words are true. I have experienced God's hand of love walk me through the darkness. During those moments in the darkness, God was working on me, purging me, teaching me, and preparing me for the next phase of giving birth to my dreams. During those times when it seemed as though there were no light in sight and I was surrounded by darkness, I discovered I was not alone. I have discovered that darkness is a good environment for God to work with you. It is a place where God has your undivided attention. It is a place where God can speak to you one-on-one. It is a place where you get up close and personal with God. It is a place where dreams and visions are illuminated in your spirit. It is a place where hope and desire serve as a light in your soul and give you strength to hold on till morning comes.

Looking back through it all, I can see how God was there with me the entire time. His hand of grace covered me. He kept my dreams burning like a light in my spirit to inspire me to press through the darkness and get to the other side. Going through the darkness strengthened and softened me in many ways. I am stronger, better, kinder, more loving, and more compassionate, and at the same time, I am more diligent, determined, focused, and excited about life, about love, and about living. It feels as though an invisible shield has been placed around me—a safeguard, a barrier, a protective force that cannot be penetrated or compromised. I feel safe. I am no longer moved or blown in the wind by other people's comments, thoughts, and opinions. My life has more meaning and purpose. I no longer feel the need to explain myself or articulate my actions. I am aware that God is the force that moves within me. It feels as though I am the passenger and God is the driver, and He is in full and complete control. I no longer feel the need to defend myself. I am no longer puzzled or bewildered by people's thoughts and opinions of me. I am no longer fazed by how people can look at me, take a sound bite of my life story, and form very strong opinions of me. I feel free. I feel loved. I am so excited about the woman I have become, and I am peaked with curiosity about what God is going to do next in my life.

I am so excited about the unfolding that is happening right before my eyes. What a lovely experience. I wish this feeling for every woman. I wish for every woman to know deep down in her spirit, she is safe, she is free, and she is loved. I feel like the seed of greatness has taken root and is getting ready to blossom into something beautiful, something magical, something powerful and life changing for me and so many women. I feel like the acorn is about to become the oak tree.

As I look back on my life and think about those people and experiences that have caused me tremendous heartache, disappointment, and pain, I can now see how those people and situations were part of my unfolding and developing story. To every person who had ill intentions or did not have my best interest in mind or chose not to do right by me, to every person who was out to get what he/she could from me, and to those individuals who misunderstood my kindness for weakness, I say thank you. Thank you for giving birth to a beautiful, wonderful, special, delicate flower. Thank you for pressing against me and allowing my potential to emerge. The pain you have caused has paved a way for me to save and heal many people around the world. Your misguided intentions have birthed a warrior, a fighter, a healer, a goddess of love and goodness. You have created a masterpiece. Thank you for every experience. Thanks to you, I have so many wonderful stories to share with the world—stories that will provide hope, peace, freedom, deliverance, and strength.

My potential has taken root, and it is going to yield a harvest of love, kindness, success, healing, and revolutionary change in so many lives around the world. God is so awesome, so amazing, and so sexy.

As I look back on my life, I am so grateful for every situation that has led me to this place, this woman. I have stumbled upon myself, and I am so excited about this discovery—another dream realized. All my life, I have never desired to be anyone else but myself. I admire many qualities about many women. I respect the essence of every woman. I applaud and celebrate every woman's uniqueness—her beauty, her style, and her being. However, my one desire has been to discover my true essence, to discover myself. Since I was little girl or as far back as I can recall, I have never wanted to be anyone, not even my mother. My mother is a beautiful, strong, kind, caring, tender, and lovely woman. She is amazing. However, I have never wanted to be her. I am my mother's daughter, and at the same time, I am my own person. I have many of my mother's features and mannerisms, and at the same time, there are many qualities and attributes about me that are uniquely mine. I have always been intrigued to discover my own wonderful uniqueness. I have always had a sense of self as long as I could remember. It's as though I have always had a crush on myself. I am totally intrigued and completely fascinated with my own existence—not in an egotistical way, but more like a healthy curiosity.

As a little girl, I set out on a quest—a journey to discover myself. I did not have a specific plan, just a strong desire and curiosity to get to know this person that is I. I did not know where to start or which direction to go, so I relied on my internal compass to show me the way. For many years, I have been searching for the woman I have become today. I have been longing to meet her, longing to know her, longing to get up close and personal with her, all sides of her—the good, the bad, and the not so pleasant. I have discovered her. She is more enchanting, kind, mysterious, loving, strong, caring, compassionate, and tender beyond my wildest imagination. I love her. I celebrate her. I honor her. Today, I am the woman I saw in my spirit many years ago. I am she; she is I. That is sexy. Thank you, God.

There are many factors that contribute to the woman I have become today and the dreams I have been blessed to see manifest in my life. I am who I am because of the wonderful people in my life—people who believe in me, support me, and love me. My two brothers are a huge part of why I am so blessed in my life. My two brothers have always believed in me. Their love for me has given me room to grow, stretch, and chase my dreams. They are very important in my life. My older brother is my guardian and my protector. My younger brother is my best friend and the person who listens to me and believes in my dreams.

When we were kids, my younger brother was my dream buddy. We would sit, talk, and dream about the big life we wanted to have once we grew up. We would talk about everything. We would sit on the front porch and play "1, 2, 3, that's my car" when a really nice car would pass by. Those were the good old days. My younger brother is a great listener. He is the kind of brother every girl should be blessed to have in her life. He is the best. No matter how crazy or outrageous my dreams, desires, and ideas appeared, my brother always listened with such intent enthusiasm and excitement. He never questioned or discouraged me. His quiet confidence made me feel as though I could do anything. His silent agreement gave me the courage to believe in myself.

My younger brother has walked alongside me as I have given birth to many of my dreams. His quiet faith gave me reassurance that I could do it. We have had some crazy, fun moments going through the "dream birthing" process. We have enjoyed laughing about walking in the unknown with blinders on. We both have witnessed my dreams transition from the unmanifested into the manifested realm. I have been blessed to experience many of my dreams, goals, and desires come to pass. I am grateful for my younger brother and his faith in me. I have seen God serve my answered prayers to me on a silver platter. I believe faith and hope, along with concentrated effort, can produce amazing things.

God has blessed me to have two amazing brothers who make me feel safe, loved, strong, beautiful, confident, and courageous. For the woman I have become and yet am becoming, I am grateful for their love and support. For such blessings, I say thank you and "I love you" to both of you.

I believe love gives us the courage to discover our wings so we can fly and soar high like eagles. As I continue on my journey, I am in awe of the power and capacity of the

You Are Enough

human spirit. I am amazed at the things I have discovered about myself, like strength, courage, and the power of forgiveness. I believe there is a seed of greatness inside every person, every woman—a seed of greatness that has no limits, no bounds. Everyone has this gift of greatness inside them. Each one of us has an internal compass that is set due north and that points toward greatness. There are gifts, talents, and qualities about you that will change the world. Through you, spirits will be healed and lives will be changed. Because of you, others will tap into their greatness. The world is counting on you to discover your gifts and talents to make a difference in the world.

Truth is, the compass within is what directs and guides us toward our unique greatness, our highest, best self. The questions to ask yourself right now are "Why am I not pursuing my dreams?" and "What thoughts am I allowing to control my mind?" Ponder these questions and allow God to reveal the answers to you so you can get unstuck, start pursuing your dreams, and discover your purpose. While pondering these questions, here is a suggestion to help clear the fog and open your spirit. I believe gratitude is the gateway to greatness. I believe cultivating a spirit of gratitude is a great way to get your compass pointed back in the right direction. I also believe it is important to express your authentic feelings as a way to release unhealthy emotions and open your spirit. I believe it is especially important to release toxic emotions and negative energy such as anger, regret, and disappointment from your spirit. Here is your assignment. Create two lists. Make the first list your thank-you list. On your thank-you list, write down the names of all the people in your life who have provided words of hope, encouragement, and love. List all the people who believed in you even when you had doubts and felt weary and lost. List all the people who saw your potential before you were aware of it. Write down the names of the individuals who saw a spark of greatness in you and planted seeds of hope and love in your spirit that helped to cultivate your confidence and your ability to believe in yourself and set you out on your journey to discover your potential. This list could consist of friends, family members, teachers, strangers, etc. Make the second list your fuck-you list. On your fuck-you list, write down the names of all the people who told you that you were less than others, names of all the people who told you that you wouldn't be anything, and names of all the people who said negative, hurtful things about you that have had a negative impact on your life. List the names of all the people who doubted your potential. Now that you have written out both lists, hold on to your thank-you list. As for your fuck-you list, say a prayer of forgiveness for all the names on the list then burn it. By writing down the names and then burning the list, you are releasing the negative energy from your mental, emotional, and spiritual space. You are cleansing and clearing your inner space so God can reveal awesome and magnificent revelations to you. Once you have done this, you should feel free, liberated, and ready to continue on your journey.

Pursuing your dreams is like taking a leap of faith into the unknown. It is like setting out on an adventure where the map is not quite clear; however, the destination is certain. Trust in your inner spirit. Have the courage to venture into the unknown; be willing to explore the many unfamiliar territories within. Decide today that you are going to write down your list of dreams and goals. Make a commitment to yourself that you are going to trust and believe in yourself. Make a declaration to yourself that you are willing to burn the boat, venture out into the unknown, and discover your greatness. Make up in your mind that you would rather drown out in the sea in search of your greatness than to continue in your current state and allow your life to pass you by. In order to get to the other side, you first have to take a step of faith. You have to get off the sideline, leave the shore, and step out in the ocean. If you are waiting for the perfect time, perfect conditions, and perfect circumstances, let me assure you, you will be waiting forever. If you don't believe me, let's take a look at how much time has gone by while you are waiting for the perfect moment to present itself. Look at how many years have gone by while you are still waiting for the ideal circumstances. Imagine how far along you could have been if you had begun your journey yesterday, last week, last month, last year, or two years ago. Just think how much sweeter your life would be right now if you had taken a leap of faith five years ago. Today is a great day, and now is the perfect time to take the leap. Make a commitment to yourself today that you are going to pursue your dreams and walk into your destiny. Remember, once you make the commitment, there is no turning back. You have to burn the boat. It is sink or swim, do or die.

Let me encourage you by saying that once you take your first step of faith, it will move God. Your first step of faith will send a strong message to God that you trust and believe in His power, wisdom, and guidance. Your act of faith of making a commitment to yourself and burning the boat will ignite the strength and courage you will need to get to the other side to realize your dreams and discover your purpose. You are not alone. Remember, you have the power within to successfully complete this journey. God has given you everything you need to get to the other side. Believe in yourself and trust God. You owe it to yourself; you owe it to your loved ones. You owe it to the world to discover your greatness. There are many people waiting on you to discover your true essence. There are many people waiting to be healed through you. There are many people hoping, believing, and trusting you will discover your true essence because your unique gifts, skills, and talents will make a difference in the world.

Today, speak words of power, hope, gratitude, and love into your life. Today, decide you are no longer a victim but a victor. You are more than a conqueror. You are no longer going to allow past situations or circumstances to limit the possibilities of your future. You are no longer going to sit down, stand by, and wait for someone to give you a hand up. You are going to ask God to give you the strength to rise up, stand tall, and become the woman He created and destined you to be. Today, you are no longer seeking approval from others. Forget and ignore what other people have said about you. Today, ask God to show you who you are, your beauty, His love for you, and all the other wonderful things about you. Today, make a commitment to yourself to be the best person/woman you can be. Today, make a decision that you are going to do whatever it takes to discover your true essence. Affirm this mantra in your heart and spirit, "Yea, though I walk through the valley of the shadow of death, I will fear no evil for God is with me. His rod and staff will comfort me, guide me, and lead me through this journey of self-discovery." Once you have burned the boat and have stepped out into the chasm of the unknown to discover your greatness within, your only responsibility is to believe and have faith in the One who created you. He will be with you every step of the way. God wants you to discover your treasure chest within. God desires and longs for you to discover your beauty, your wisdom, your strength, and your power.

There is a fire that burns within each of us—a fire that lights the path that leads each individual to his/her own greatness. We all have this fire inside us. There is no person without this burning fire within. The question is, will you believe in yourself enough to venture within into the unknown? Will you allow the fire within to burn away your insecurities, doubts, and issues of your past? Will you allow the fire within to purify you and take you to places beyond your wildest dreams? Will you allow the fire within to slough off all those unnecessary, unwanted edges of poor self-esteem and low self-image? Will you allow the fire within to sharpen you, prepare you, and take you to places that will blow your mind? If you will keep the faith and press forward, then your dreams will come to pass. God will blow your mind and change your life right before your eyes.

    I am a living witness that dreams do come true. I believe in you. Have faith and believe in yourself. Your dreams can come true. I believe a little faith can take you a long way in life and I believe a lot of faith can take you into this realm called heaven on earth. So pursue your dreams, have faith, and trust God. You have what it takes to make your dreams a reality. Take a moment to sit quietly with yourself and reflect on the dreams you are holding in your heart; decide you are going to pursue your dreams, then complete the declaration on the next page.

My Declaration

I, _____, promise to believe in myself and walk in faith.

I, _____, commit to seeing my dreams become reality.

I, _____, believe I have greatness within.

Chapter 5

Value / Guard Your Time

Next to love, time is the most precious commodity in life. Your time should be highly respected and guarded. Be mindful of whom you give your time, your attention, and your energy to. Treat your time like a precious coin. Invest your time in ways that will yield positive returns. For example, spend time giving hope, encouragement, and love to others, and spend time with the people you love. Take time to tell your family and loved ones how much their love means to you. Set aside time to spend one-on-one quality moments with your children. The one-on-one time invested with your children will yield huge returns. Children who are loved and nurtured usually grow up to be happy, productive, responsible, and well-rounded adults.

Also, another way to value your time is to invest time in young people who do not have a positive role model in their lives. Take time out of your life and give it to a young person who needs it. This act of kindness is like planting seeds in fertile soil. Quality time spent with a young person could yield a beautiful return. Quality time invested in a young person could change that young person's life and put the young person's life on a totally different course—a course toward greatness. Quality time invested in a young person could be a source of love, attention, and consistency the child needs to find his or her way in the world. This wise investment of your time could yield huge dividends. The bottom line is, you have the right to use your time however you see fit. Whether you choose to use your time wisely and sensibly is your choice.

Here is a reality check: time spent is time gone, so make sure you are investing your precious time on situations and people that are worth it. You have the right to own your life and time. You have every right to decide who and what is worthy of your time. You do not owe anyone an explanation for how you spend your time. Time waits for no one. If you think I am making this up, try this on for size: Can you go back and capture the time that has passed since you picked up this book? Here is another reality check. Time keeps on ticking with or without you. Whether you choose to show up in your life and be fully present daily is a choice. This is a very powerful and empowering gift you have been given. Many people lay down last night and transitioned into a permanent slumber. Today, you are still here. Today, you have been granted another opportunity to show up for yourself, to get busy living, to put the past in its place (in the past and behind you), and to focus on being grateful right now. You have been given another opportunity to create the life you would like to have. Time is precious. Now is a great time to get started living with purpose and passion.

Just in case you are reading this book and thinking to yourself, *The writer does not understand what I have been through. The writer does not understand how much pain I felt from the divorce or the breakup. The writer has no clue how difficult it is just to get out of bed due to being held in the grips of depression,* or you are saying, "The writer does not understand all the odds stacked against me right now. She does not understand that my situation is too overwhelming for me to handle or overcome." Well, let me just say that I may not understand the specifics of your life's circumstances, but I can tell you I have had my share of heartaches, disappointments, setbacks, and slammed doors. I have experienced my share of moments when I have felt lost and hopeless. I have had many moments when I have questioned why I am here. I have asked God if my life has any real meaning and purpose. I have put myself in some unhappy and compromised situations where my life was hanging in the balance. Just like you, I have had my share of questions, doubts, unhappy thoughts, and feelings; however, with each situation, I was aware that I always had a choice—a choice to make a different decision, a choice to change my perspective. As long as I was granted the gift of time to see another day, I believed there was hope for a new beginning, another chance to change my life and my circumstances.

The gift of time and the power to choose have led me to write this book and to this wonderful juncture in my life—a beautiful and amazing life! Just like some people who will read this book, I have had a few close calls with death as a result of not valuing my time and of making poor choices. As a matter of fact, I have learned firsthand the value of guarding my time. I have felt the intense feeling of being face-to-face with what seemed like my final hour. Many moons ago, in my midtwenties, I experienced a situation where my life flashed right before my eyes as a result of another person's anger and rage and as a result of making poor choices. I have felt the feeling of the clock about to run out—my last hour, the end. The experience I am about to share with you was a blessing in disguise. The experience served as a huge wake-up call, a loud shout to get my attention—a thunderous clap to wake me up and get my life in focus. I am sharing my story in hopes that you will learn from my experience and avoid wasting time and putting your life in harm's way.

Here is what happened. Many years ago, I was going out with this guy. His name is not important, just the details of the story. When I met the guy, I was not looking for a serious relationship. I had recently gotten out of a long-term relationship. I told the guy I needed time to thaw out and recover mentally, spiritually, and emotionally from my recent relationship. I explained to him that I was emotionally unavailable and just wanted to hang out and have fun. I was not interested in pursuing a serious relationship with the guy. He was a nice guy, but he was not the "meet the family" type of guy. He was just a distraction—something fun to do for the moment. The guy decided he still wanted to hang out with me. Here is where I did not set a proper boundary. I allowed him to pursue me, take me out, and wine and dine me. I did not respect my time or his time. I was caught up in the moment of being emotionally numb and wanting to just have fun to keep my mind and thoughts off the lingering hurt and pain in my heart. In the beginning, things were very carefree and fun. He took me to nice restaurants; he made me laugh. Whenever I wanted to hang out, he was available. In my mind, we were two people spending time together, just hanging out. After some time, I became bored and less interested in the guy. I met new friends—a group of really cool girls and guys. I began to spend more time with my new friends and less time with the guy. I really enjoyed spending time with my new friends, so this meant less time spent with the guy. This did not go over well with him. He began calling obsessively, leaving messages, and calling at weird hours late in the night. I ignored his calls for weeks.

After some time, the calls and messages stopped. I assumed he had gotten the picture that our situation had changed and I was no longer interested in hanging out with him on a regular basis anymore. Remember, earlier I stated I told him I was not looking for a commitment or a relationship. Oh, let me go back a bit and explain what happened while we were hanging out and having fun. Over the course of time of us getting to know each other, he received a large sum of money from an "insurance settlement." I believe the money was from some sort of drug deal. I was never certain of his occupation. He was usually available when I wanted to hang out. On a few occasions, he was not available to hang out because he had to work the night shift, supposedly. It was a weird situation. When he asked me if I could keep the money from the insurance settlement for him, I said okay. He gave me $10,000 cash to hold until further notice or until he needed it. He said I could spend as much as I would like to spend. His only request was that I not spend all the money. Well, I'm a girl who loves to shop, and that's all I'm going to say about that.

Moving on, after things changed between us and I began hanging out with my new friends, he ceased with the obsessive calling and messages. I figured he had gotten the picture and had moved on. Not so much, several weeks had gone by, and I had not heard from him, so I felt I no longer needed to screen my calls. Well, one afternoon, out of the blue, he called. I answered the phone; he was calm, mild, and pleasant. He had called to tell me someone had broken into his home and had stolen most of his belongings, including all his television sets. He asked if he could come over and borrow the spare TV that was in my closet. I said, "Sure." Later that evening, I had plans to go out on a date with a new friend. The plan was for the guy to stop by around 6:30 p.m. to pick up the TV before

I went out on my date for 7:00 p.m. When the guy arrived at my place, I opened the door and greeted him. My plan was to let him grab the TV out of the closet near the front door as I grabbed my purse from the sofa. Things did not quite unfold as planned. As I turned my back to grab my purse off the couch, because my plan was for it to be a quick pickup and go and for us to walk out at the same time, in a moment, things escalated to something I did not see coming. When I turned back around from grabbing my purse from the sofa, he was standing in front of me with a gun pointed in my face. At first, it was as though I were dreaming. I thought to myself, *This cannot be happening right now because I have a date.* (Talk about not being fully present in the moment.) He pointed the gun at me. He nudged me back inside; he closed the front door and forced me to sit on the sofa, and he read me my rights. He told me how angry he was that I had not returned any of his calls and had ignored his numerous requests to hang out. He was pissed. He was angry. He had death in his eyes. He had come to kill me for causing him so much pain, and he was prepared to take his own life. He stated he was tired of being hurt, and he said he was not going to jail after killing me, so he was prepared to take his life after shooting and killing me. Looking back, what's interesting is that I was not afraid. I guess I was numb or in shock. There was one comment he made that sort of jolted me. He mentioned he had attempted to find my mother's phone number in the white pages earlier that day. He said he wanted to call my mother and tell her he was coming over to kill her daughter. This really got my attention, not so much that he was going to kill me, but the thought of fear and terror this news would have caused my mother. The thought of him calling my mother disturbed me more than the gun he had pointed in my face. My mother loves all three of her children more than she loves her own life. I know this news would have killed her of a heart attack. She would have died. The mere thought of her worrying about me made me snap into reality. I remember looking into the guy's eyes. I remember his eyes being cold, empty, and dark. His eyes looked like death. He said it was going to be the end for both of us that night because he was going to kill himself after he shot and killed me. It seemed he had planned things out, and there I was, caught up in the drama I had created as a result of not valuing my precious time or his time.

From the start, I knew I was not interested in anything serious with him, yet I allowed myself to get caught up in a situation that almost cost me my life. The short version of the long story is, for hours, I sat apologizing to the guy for hurting, misleading, and taking him for granted. I must have said "I'm sorry" a thousand times. It seemed the more I said "I'm sorry" to him, the more I could see life coming back into his eyes. I could see the anger and tension breaking inside him. Things unfolded; he said his peace, and I apologized numerous times. I gave him the remainder of his money, and we both moved on.

My life was spared, thank goodness. This was a huge lesson. I almost lost my life, and I wasted precious, valuable time getting caught up in a situation that I knew from the beginning was not going anywhere.

I hope you will learn from my mistakes and have the courage and good common sense to value your time and not allow yourself to get caught up in a situation that could cost you your life. If you are reading this book and you are in your twenties or thirties, take my advice: do not waste your time on people or situations you consciously know are not worth your time. Have the inner resolve and respect to walk away from unhealthy relationships and situations. If you are in your forties or fifties, do not waste your time worrying about things you cannot change. Let it go, move on, and live your life to the fullest. Do not allow past regrets to rob you of precious time. Live in the moment! Value your time, learn from your mistakes, and keep your head held high. Focus your time and energy on living your dreams, discovering your purpose, and making the most of this beautiful gift called life.

Use your time wisely. Create positive, healthy moments that will linger in your spirit and stay with you. In spite of the crazy, frustrating, difficult things that are happening in your life, strive to create rich and delicious memories that will linger in your spirit forever.

Today, my life is an adventure. I am blessed to have had so many extraordinary experiences in my life. I have experienced moments that have melted my heart to a puddle of mush. I have enjoyed moments that have taken my breath away. The remnants of those wonderful experiences still linger in my spirit like deliciously fragranced flowers. Such moments are simply divine. I can still feel the warm, tender, and spiritual feeling I felt when my lover prepared a footbath for me. The footbath was perfectly prepared with warm water and lovely lavender-scented salts. I can still see him as he carefully placed my feet into the foot massage tub and gently washed my feet while kneeling on his knees. He was so caring and so attentive. The moment was special, beautiful, and sacred. I have also had some experiences that were so exhilarating that my senses were overloaded with joy and excitement. I can still feel the feeling I felt when I went skydiving several years ago. I can still recall the moment leading up to jumping out of the airplane and the overwhelming rush of exhilaration coursing through my body when I first jumped out of the plane thirteen thousand feet in the sky. I can recall the amazingly calm and serene feeling I felt once the parachute opened and we stabilized in the air. It was an awesome experience. Take time to be present in your life. Treasure your life. Guard your time. Live your life with meaning, purpose, and passion. Wake up, slow down, and savor each moment. Don't let life pass you by, and don't allow yourself to be so busy doing that you fail to take time to live, feel, experience, and enjoy life. Seek to experience the fullness of each moment. Tell yourself, "I must enjoy this special moment right now because it will not pass my way again." Take a moment to sit quietly with yourself and reflect on how you are currently spending your time; decide who and what is worthy of your time, then complete the declaration on the next page.

My Declaration

I, _____, promise to spend my time wisely. I, _____, commit to using my time to make a difference in the world. I, _____, believe my time is valuable, and I will treat it as such.

Conclusion

Life is a beautiful and amazing journey. How you choose to live it is entirely up to you. You have the power and right to choose the quality of your life. I hope the words in this book have inspired, motivated, and challenged you. I hope you now understand that who you are is enough. You are special. You are beautiful. You are a masterpiece. There is so much goodness and greatness inside you.

I hope this book has offered some form of healing of your past and hope for a brighter and better future. I hope you have come to understand that you are not other people's opinion of you. I hope you have been inspired to live with purpose and passion. The world needs you. The world needs your gifts, your skills, your talents, and your love. There are people waiting to be healed through you. You are someone's healing. You have work to do, my beloved. Your life and your story are going to bless, inspire, and encourage so many women. So wake up and get present in your life. Get motivated to go after your dreams. Be inspired to discover your purpose. No more excuses, no more acting like a victim, no more blaming other people for your current state. No more excuses for your lack of courage. You are ready. God is ready. The world is ready and waiting on you.

Get started now, rise from the ashes, burn the boat, and walk in faith toward your new life. Watch God do some awesome and amazing things in your life.

I am excited for you and looking forward to all the wonderful things that are about to happen in your life. I want you to know that dreams do come true. Your life does matter. You are important. You are special. You are loved. May the light of love lead you, guide you, and usher you into your promised land. I am cheering for you. Life is grand.

About the Author

Jacqueline is a human resources professional with fifteen-plus years' experience. She is a motivational speaker and empowerment consultant. Jacqueline facilitates empowerment workshops and hosts group discussions that are exciting, engaging, and interactive. Her group discussions are very popular. Guests walk away from her workshops feeling enlightened, informed, and empowered. Her most popular discussions are "Girl Talk" and "Dinner, Wine, and Conversation."

Jacqueline believes there are no limits in life, only limited thinking. People waste lots of mental space and precious time dwelling on old dead past situations and events. She believes most people are standing in their own way, sabotaging their own happiness, and thwarting their own potential.

Every person has the power and capacity to change his or her life by renewing his or her mind and developing a new set of skills, tools, and strategies that will have a direct and positive impact on his or her quality of life. Each person was created with special, unique gifts that are buried deep inside a treasure chest within—gifts that were meant to be discovered and given to the world.

Index

A

abilities, 6, 8-9, 56
acceptance, complete, 13
adventure, personal, 9
anger, 33, 38-39, 55, 69
anxiety, 11-12, 36, 47

B

beliefs, 3, 7-8, 13, 24, 48
Bible, 7, 22, 26-27
blessing, 10, 12, 38, 54, 65
boundaries, 11, 19, 33-34, 66

C

change, xv, 10-11, 33, 52
choices, 6, 14, 17-18, 20, 33, 39, 64-65
college education, 47-48
commitment, xv, 7, 12, 21, 26-27, 33, 35, 56-58, 67
compassion, xv, 1-2
courage, x, xiv, 11-12, 14, 21, 31, 33-34, 36, 48-49, 54-57, 69, 76
Creator, xii, xiv-xv, 1, 3, 10, 14, 25, 43
curiosity, 25, 27, 51, 53

D

darkness, x, 50-51
decisions, 12, 17-18, 20-21, 33-34, 58, 65
declaration, 14-15, 28-29, 33, 39, 41, 56, 59, 61, 71, 73
deliverance, 52
difference, 44, 55, 58, 73
disciple course, 26-27

discovery, xiv, 12, 25, 27, 36, 52
dream birthing process, 49, 54
dream buddy, 54
dream realizers, 43
dreams, 20-21, 43-45, 48-50, 52-57, 59, 61, 70, 75-76

E

ego, 37
encouragement, 21, 55, 63
energy, 20, 33-34, 63, 70
engine of change, 17
entanglements, 39
essence, true, 10, 13, 15, 24, 31, 52, 57-58
excitement, x, 8, 19, 26-27, 47, 54, 70
existence, 17-18, 22, 44, 53
experience, ix, xii, 9, 25, 27, 36, 45-48, 51-52, 65-66, 70

F

faith, xi, 10-11, 14, 21, 43-49, 54, 57-59, 61, 76
force, xi, 9, 20, 27, 44, 51
forgiveness, xii, 38-39, 55-56
freedom, iii, x, xiv, 2, 13-14, 19, 39, 52
friendships, xiii, 33

G

gifts, 2, 8-9, 13-14, 19, 25, 55, 58, 65, 75
God, 3-5, 13, 22-27, 34-38, 46-59, 65, 76
grace, 1-2, 5-6, 38, 50
gratitude, 48, 55, 58
greatness, 1, 51, 55-58, 61, 64, 75
guidance, 47, 49, 57

H

happiness, 18, 44, 77
hate, 38-39
healing, xi, xv, 12, 22, 35-37, 39, 52, 75
hope, ix-xii, 21-22, 24, 28, 38, 47-50, 52, 54-56, 58, 63, 65
hurt, xii, 6, 39, 66

I

invitation, ix-xi, 38, 43, 46

J

Jesus, 22-23, 27
journey, xi-xii, xv, 2, 10, 24-25, 34-35, 38, 48, 53-54, 56-57
  of discovery, 25, 36
  of self-discovery, 27, 58

joy, iii, x, 1, 8, 18, 26, 44, 50, 70

K

kindness, 37, 52, 63

L

life, 2-5, 8-13, 17-22, 25-29, 31, 33-34, 37-39, 41, 43-45, 48-49, 51-57, 63-66, 68-71, 75-76
light, 13-14, 44, 48, 50-51, 58, 76
list
  of dreams, 21, 56
  fuck-you, 56
  thank-you, 55
love, 1-2, 6-9, 12-14, 24, 27-28, 39, 54-56, 58, 63-64

M

masterpiece, ix, 52, 75
meditation, 36-37
mind, ix-xi, 3-4, 7-8, 12, 18, 21, 23-24, 32-37, 39, 44, 46-47, 49, 52, 55-56, 59, 66, 77
Mississippi, 22, 24, 45-46

O

Opinion, 31-32, 34, 38-39, 41, 75

P

pain, xi, 10, 38-39, 51-52, 64, 66, 68
passion, 2, 17, 20, 64, 71, 75
past, ix-xi, 17, 38, 58-59, 64, 75
patience, 1, 37, 49-50
peace, iii, 1, 8, 11-12, 18, 28, 50, 52, 69
possibilities, 17, 19-20, 44-45, 48, 58
potential, 18, 27, 29, 35, 43, 45, 49, 52, 55-56
power, x, 1-2, 6-9, 18, 20-21, 26-27, 29, 31-32, 34-35, 37-39, 41, 44-45, 54-55, 57-58, 65, 75, 77
prayer, 11, 22, 47, 56
preacher, 23-24
prison, self-created, 14, 18
promised land, x, 25, 76
protector, 5, 53
purpose, special, 7, 9, 34, 37

Q

qualities, 8, 12, 34, 52-53, 55, 75

R

relationships, xi, 4, 11, 20-21, 33, 39, 44, 69
release, xi-xii, 20
responsibility, ix, 2, 5, 14, 17-18, 32, 58

S

scripture, 7, 26
self, true, 10, 13, 36
self-love, 6, 8, 12
sexiness, xv, 12-13
soul, x, xii, 7, 38, 50
Source, 2-3, 26, 31
Southern University and A&M College, 47-48
specialness, 11-12
spirit, ix-xii, 2, 4, 7-8, 10-13, 19-20, 23-25, 27-28, 32, 34-36, 38-39, 44, 46-51, 53, 55-56, 58, 70
stories, Bible, 22, 24-25
strength, xv, 12, 21, 31, 34, 49-50, 52, 55, 57-58
support, xv, 46-47, 53-54

T

taskmaster, 23
thoughts
  self-defeating, 33, 35
  self-hating, 6
  self-sabotaging, 33
  toxic, 11
time, 33, 64, 69-70
treasure, 2, 4, 58, 71
treasure chest, 9, 12-13, 58, 77
trust, xi, 39
truth, ix, 3, 6-7, 25-26, 35, 55

U

unfolding, 51
uniqueness, ix, xv, 53

W

wisdom, xiii, xv, 2, 9, 11-13, 22, 24-26, 48-50, 57-58
women, xv, 2-3, 8, 14, 31, 34-35, 51-52, 75
world
  inner, 8
  physical, 45